THE BLACK WIDOW SPIDER

BY
NANCY J. NIELSEN

EDITED BY
JULIE BACH

CRESTWOOD HOUSE
New York

LIBRARY OF CONGRESS CATALOGING IN PUBLICATION DATA

Nielsen, Nancy J.
 The black widow spider

 (Wildlife, habits & habitat)
 Includes index.
 SUMMARY: Examines the physical characteristics, behavior, and natural environment of the black widow spider.
 1. Black widow spider—Juvenile literature.   [1. Black widow spider.   2. Spiders.]   I. Title.   II. Series.
 QL458.42.T54N54   1990   595.4'4—dc20   89-28271
 ISBN 0-89686-513-4

PHOTO CREDITS:

Cover: DRK Photo: (Stephen J. Krasemann)
Photo Researchers: (James H. Carmichael, Jr.) 4; (John Serrao) 7; (James H. Robinson) 8, 14, 19, 22, 24, 26, 28; (Larry Miller) 11; (Joseph T. Collins) 20; (J.P. Jackson) 21; (S. Greenberg) 25; (William M. Partington) 31; (Stephen J. Krasemann) 34-35; (Robert Lee) 44-45
DRK Photo: (Dick Canby) 10; (Leonard Lee Rue III) 38
Berg & Associates: (Kenneth L. Weaver) 41

Copyright © 1990 by Crestwood House, Macmillan Publishing Company

All rights reserved. No part of this book may be reproduced or transmitted in any form or by any means, electronic or mechanical, including photocopying, recording, or by any information storage and retrieval system, without permission in writing from the Publisher.

Macmillan Publishing Company
866 Third Avenue
New York, NY 10022
Collier Macmillan Canada, Inc.

Printed in the United States of America
First Edition
10 9 8 7 6 5 4 3 2 1

TABLE OF CONTENTS

Introduction: America's most poisonous spider 5
Chapter I: The black widow in close-up 6
    A spider is not an insect
    Spiders, spiders everywhere
    What does a black widow look like?
Chapter II: The black widow stays close to home 16
    Where do black widows live?
    A tangled web
    The black widow has enemies, too
Chapter III: The black widow's life cycle 21
    Courtship and mating
    Egg sacs
    Ballooning
    Molting
Chapter IV: What's for supper? 29
    A black widow eats almost anything
    A web makes a happy hunting ground
    The black widow keeps a tidy web
Chapter V: The black widow and humans 36
    Spidermania
    Black widows can be helpful
    Preventing black widow bites
    What to do if you are bitten
Index/Glossary 46–47

INTRODUCTION:

A grasshopper leaps into a black widow spider's web and becomes tangled in it. Out darts a large female black widow spider. She has been hiding in a dark corner of her web. The grasshopper, which is much larger than the black widow, struggles to get loose. But the black widow uses her *silk* as rope to tie the grasshopper more tightly into the web. If the black widow feels her life is in danger, she will also bite the grasshopper with her *fangs,* shooting poison into it. Once the grasshopper is dead, the black widow will settle down to a juicy dinner.

Even the black widow's own mate is afraid of her. The male, who enters her web only to mate, is three or more times smaller than the female. If he climbs onto her web when she is hungry or in a bad mood, she may eat him for dinner. No wonder she is called the black *widow*.

Female black widow spiders also may bite humans who surprise or disturb them. The male black widow is too small to bite through human skin, but poison from a female black widow can make a person ill. In some cases, it even causes death. The female black widow is America's most poisonous spider.

Have you ever seen a black widow spider? Do you know what one looks like? Because her bite is such a deadly one, it is a good idea to know as much as you can about her.

After binding this grasshopper to its web, the black widow spider will probably eat it for dinner.

CHAPTER ONE:

We do not know much about the *evolution* of the black widow spider, or of spiders in general. That's because we learn about animal pasts by reading *fossils*, and not many spiders have been fossilized. We do know, however, that spiders have been around about 400 million years longer than humans have!

A spider is not an insect

Because of its size, many people think a spider is just another insect. This is not so, although both insects and spiders belong to the same *phylum*, called *Arthropoda*. Crabs, shrimp, centipedes, scorpions, ticks, and mites also belong to this phylum. Spiders belong to a class called *Arachnida*. Insects are in a class of their own.

You can easily tell a spider from an insect by counting its legs. Insects have six legs; spiders have eight legs. Also, insects have wings, but spiders do not.

An insect's body is made up of three different parts. A spider's body has only two parts: the *cephalothorax* (head and chest) and the *abdomen*.

The cephalothorax of a spider is covered with a hard shell, similar to that of a lobster. The cephalothorax con-

All spiders, including the black widow, have eight legs and two body parts—an abdomen and a cephalothorax.

A black widow's pedipalps help the spider move along its web and feed itself.

tains the spider's brain, nervous system, mouth, and sucking stomach. Extending in front are a spider's special plierlike jaws, called *chelicerae*. They include the fangs, which are connected to the poison glands. On top are the spider's eyes; a black widow has eight.

Just outside the chelicerae are the *pedipalps*, often called palps for short. They may look like antennae, but they function more like feelers. The palps help the spider find its way and move food to its mouth. A male's palps are much larger than a female's because he sometimes stores a fluid called *sperm* in them.

All eight legs are attached to the cephalothorax. A spider's legs are similar to the legs of an insect, except that they have one extra joint. If a young spider loses a leg, it can grow another one. Behind the cephalothorax is the spider's abdomen. It contains the heart, lungs, and digestive tube. A female's abdomen is much larger than a male's because she must have room to store her eggs.

Also located in the abdomen are the *silk glands*. Different glands are used for making different kinds of silk. The glands are connected to tiny pores called *spinnerets*. These stick out of the spider's tail. The silk is spun into strands through the spinnerets. Two claws and a hook that help the spider stay on its web are also located at the tail.

Spiders and insects differ in other ways, too. Insects cannot spin webs, as most spiders do. Insects eat plants, but spiders eat only other animals, usually insects. Insects have *compound eyes* and good vision. Spiders do not see very well.

Spiders, spiders everywhere

Spiders seem to be almost everywhere. They live in deserts and jungles, wilderness areas and houses. The house spider is the most common kind of spider, and it is harmless to humans.

Scientists have discovered about 100,000 *species* of spi-

The tarantula, which is the largest spider found in the United States, has a sting like that of a bee.

ders. Only about 20,000 of these live in the United States. The largest spiders live in China. They are almost as big as birds. The *tarantula* is the largest spider found in the United States. It looks scary, but is actually rather harmless. Other spiders are so tiny they can barely be seen.

Most spiders are poisonous, but few of them have fangs large enough to bite through human skin. Of those that can, only two spiders in the United States are dangerous to humans. They are the brown recluse and the black widow. The recluse is found in the southern states. Its bite is painful and may cause a blister. The blister may take more than three months to heal.

All black widow spiders belong to a family called *Theridiidae*, the comb-footed spiders. They are known for the irregular tangled webs they weave. Only the fe-

The brown recluse spider is one species of poisonous spiders found in the United States. This brown recluse works on its egg sac.

The habitat of the black widow spider

male widow spiders from this family are poisonous to humans.

Different species of widow spiders live in many areas of the world. (Their scientific name, or *genus*, is *Latrodectus*, which means "a biting robber.") In Mexico, the widow spider is called *araña capulina*, or "cherry spider." In Russia, the widow is called "black wolf spider." The

South African widow is named "shoe button spider," while New Zealanders call their widow the "night stinger." In Australia, the widow is referred to as the "red-black spider."

Five different species of widow spiders live in the United States. The brown widow is a brown tropical spider and can be found only in southern Florida. The red widow also lives in Florida. It has reddish legs and its abdomen has bright red spots. The other three kinds of widows in the United States are black widow spiders.

What does a black widow look like?

Mature female black widows are a shiny black color with red markings on their bellies. Males and young females can be brown or black with red, orange, or yellow stripes or markings. The abdomen of the mature female is about the size of a pea.

The three species of black widow in the United States are *Latrodectus mactans, Latrodectus variolus*, and *Latrodectus hesperus*. It is difficult to tell which species a female belongs to, especially as she gets older. The males are easier to identify.

L. mactans is the most common species of black

widow, especially in the southern states. Its red belly markings form the shape of an hourglass. The female's legs are unmarked, but the male has stripes on his legs and three white stripes on his abdomen.

L. variolus is much less common, but can be found farther north, even into Canada. The two halves of the hourglass marking on the belly are separated. The female has white spots on her neck. The male has four instead of three white stripes, and the stripes are broader than those of *L. mactans*.

L. hesperus is found in the western half of the United States and into Canada. It also has a completed red hourglass marking on its belly. Instead of the white markings of *L. variolus*, both male and female have olive-gray or pink markings.

L. mactans is a bit smaller than the other two species. In general, though, a male black widow is about 4 millimeters long when measured from its front legs to its back legs. It weighs between 8 and 18 milligrams. The female is about 12 millimeters long and weighs 120 to 400 milligrams. But once a researcher found a female black widow that weighed 945 milligrams. That's 65 times the weight of the average male.

The three species of black widow look very similar. But if a spider is about the size of a pea and is shiny black with red markings on its belly, it is probably a female black widow.

The female black widow has an hourglass marking on its belly. The male, on the top, is smaller and has red and white markings.

CHAPTER TWO:

Black widows never travel too far from home. When old enough, they leave their nests by floating away on the wind. Then they build webs wherever they land. Female black widows rarely leave their web sites.

Where do black widows live?

Black widow spiders can live almost anywhere. They are most common in the southern states, but they have been found in every state except Alaska. They like grassy areas. They have been found in wheat and oat fields, in stacks of hay, between bales of cotton, in the hollows of trees, and under stones and logs.

Many black widows live close to and even inside of homes. They like dark, damp areas such as basements or attics. You might also find them lurking in barns, garages, or toolsheds, behind shutters, among loose bricks, and in woodpiles. Inside houses, black widows hide in closets, under steps, and on porches. They can lurk in baskets or shoe boxes, among stored linens, or between old books on bookshelves.

Black widow spiders can live in a variety of climates. Even though they prefer mild climates, they survive in the hottest areas of the United States. They live in the Mohave and Colorado deserts, Imperial Valley and Needles, California, and in parts of Death Valley. If a place has enough insects to supply them with food, black widows can live there.

Black widows also can survive fairly well in cold weather. They have been spotted in Denver year-round. A live black widow was once taken from a pile of tumbleweed after a heavy snowstorm.

Widows in cold weather become *torpid*, or inactive and numb to feeling. People think they survive winters because they can live for a long time without eating. But a sudden cold snap that brings temperatures below zero degrees Fahrenheit can kill them.

Black widow spiders also live in wet and humid areas such as northern California, Louisiana, Mississippi, Alabama, and the Carolinas.

A tangled web

When you think of a spider web, you may think of the beautiful *orb* web spun by Charlotte, the spider in the book *Charlotte's Web* by E. B. White. But the black widow spider weaves a different sort of web called a *tangled web*. Both males and females weave webs, but the male leaves his web when he reaches maturity.

Tangled webs are usually two sheetlike decks connected

with webbing. The webbing acts as a stairway. The webs come in a variety of shapes and sizes, depending on where they are built. The most common black widow webs are about one foot tall. One of the largest webs ever found was in a toolshed. It was twelve feet high.

The black widow starts its web with a strand of silk called a *bridge*. The rest of the web hangs from this bridge, although it is attached at the sides to other objects for support. Underneath the bridge lies the top deck. A second deck is usually built near the ground.

The silk strands in the decks are woven closely together. They are very sticky. The strands that make up the stairway are thicker and stronger, although all silk is extremely strong.

The black widow builds its web near a pile of dirt or a crack in a brick or log. It uses the crack as a hiding place. It stays there until an insect gets caught in its web. Then it scuttles out to prepare the insect for dinner.

Spiders are constantly mending their webs. Any disturbance can damage the fragile nets. Also, new silk is stickier than old silk and makes better traps.

Have you ever wondered why a spider doesn't get caught in its own web? It doesn't get caught because it has special claws and a hook at its tail. Silk will not stick to the hook. A spider grasps the silk strand with that hook. It can also loosen itself from the strand in a fraction of a second.

The claws have tiny hairs that direct the silk onto the hook. To keep its claws from sticking to the web, a spider

The mud dauber wasp is one of the black widow's worst enemies.

must clean them. It does this by drawing each leg up to its mouth to moisten each claw with saliva.

The black widow has enemies, too

You would think other animals would stay away from the deadly female black widow. But she has enemies, too.

Perhaps her worst enemy is the *mud dauber wasp*. Mud daubers do not live in colonies, as most wasps do. They live alone and hunt spiders, including the black widow. A mud dauber paralyzes, but does not kill, the black widow. Then the wasp stores the widow in an earthen cell made of mud. After filling a cell with paralyzed spiders, the

mud dauber lays an egg and closes the cell. When the egg hatches, the wasp *grub* feasts on the paralyzed spiders.

The alligator lizard also attacks black widow spiders. So do some spider-eating spiders. Mealworms have been known to eat black widows that are still young or ones that are dying. Parasitic flies and maggots will feast on black widow eggs.

In spite of her reputation, the black widow is really a shy creature. She is slow moving and does not seek out animals to attack. It is not possible to force a black widow to bite; she will do so only if frightened or alarmed. A black widow will retreat from danger when she can. Or she will curl up into a little ball and play dead.

The alligator lizard also preys on the black widow.

A female black widow lives about one year.

CHAPTER THREE:

Black widows take good care of their eggs. But once the young spiders, or *spiderlings*, hatch, they no longer need their mothers. About eight times more males than females hatch from one egg sac. Yet more females live to become adults. Males mature faster than females, but they only live about four months. Females often live a year or longer.

During a courtship, the male black widow cautiously approaches the female, who stays on her web.

Courtship and mating

During courtship, the male black widow approaches the female on her own territory and often takes his life into his hands. But if he doesn't mate, no new spiderlings will hatch.

When the male is ready to mate, he spins a small mat on which to place his sperm. The sperm contains the seeds needed to fertilize the female's eggs. Then the male collects his sperm in special pouches in his palps. Now he is ready to search for a female black widow.

A male knows a female's web by the kind of silk it is made of. Cautiously, he steps up onto her web. His abdomen starts to *vibrate*, sending a special signal to the female through the silk strands. He plucks the silk strands with his legs, also causing them to vibrate. Then he waits for an answer.

If the female is not ready to mate, the male's presence may make her angry. Then he must run for his life. If the female is not mature enough to mate, the male may simply decide to wait nearby. If the female is ready to mate, she sends the male a vibration that lets him know he can come nearer.

As the male approaches, he cuts and gathers the strand of silk on which he travels. Perhaps he does this to trap the female so she cannot escape. Sometimes the female charges at him, and he is forced to retreat. Then after a short rest, he may try again. If the female continues to charge at him, he may have to stop courting her. But if she lets him, he can be close enough to touch her in about 30 minutes.

When the male reaches the female, he tries to please her by rubbing her legs and abdomen. She may rub his legs, too. Then the male throws a loosely woven web over her.

After about two hours, the male climbs up onto her belly to a spot just underneath her deadly fangs and deposits the sperm stored in his palps. Now he must leave immediately. Otherwise, she may eat him. If the female is not hungry, though, she may allow the male to live in her web for a few days. Soon after mating, the male will die.

Egg sacs

The fertilized eggs grow inside the female's abdomen. They make her look swollen. Soon she puts them into egg sacs. The whole process takes her about two and a half hours.

After mating, the male quickly leaves the female's web, before she can eat him.

This pregnant female will soon deposit her eggs inside the egg sac attached to her web.

The egg sacs are made from silk and have a tough, papery texture. They are creamy yellow, tan, or gray and are about 12 millimeters high. A female will make as many as nine egg sacs. Each sac contains about 250 eggs. She attaches the sacs to her web, usually in an out-of-sight spot close to her retreat.

After the eggs have been deposited in the sacs, the female spins another covering for each sac made of a gauzy

As many as 250 black widow spiderlings develop inside one egg sac.

silk. This covering is twice as large as the first egg sac. It will give the spiderlings room to grow. Then she spends much time covering it with a tough silk for further protection.

The female black widow protects her eggs in times of danger. She does this by holding on to them with her front legs. She also moves her sacs about to keep them safe from the sun and the rain.

After a couple of weeks, the eggs are ready to hatch. Each egg is about one millimeter high and is rubbery in texture. If dropped, the eggs will bounce.

As the spiderlings outgrow their shells, they gradually push out of them. Then they feed on their shells and on each other.

The baby spiders have no eyes or hair. Within a couple of days, though, these start to grow. The spiderlings are clear and rubbery like the fake spiders found in toy stores. The spiderlings do not have any markings yet. It is not possible to tell male and female spiderlings apart.

Soon the spiderlings are ready to leave the egg sac. They tear a hole in the outer covering and crawl out onto it. The female black widow may eat many of her young before they have a chance to leave home.

Ballooning

Spiderlings have an interesting way of leaving home. First they crawl to the top of a weed or fence. Then they face the wind, stretch out their legs, and tilt their abdomens up toward the sky. The wind pulls long strands of silk thread from the young spiders' spinnerets. As soon as the threads are long and strong enough to support them, the wind carries them away to their new homes. This process is called *ballooning*.

Spiderlings seem to travel with air currents even on days when the wind is still. On windy days, they can travel long distances. Even adult spiders are sometimes carried away by strong winds.

Once the spiders land, they build webs. Living alone as they do, black widows don't have to compete with one another for food. Still young, the spiderlings must eat and grow a lot before they become adults.

Molting

A spiderling grows through a process called *molting*. Its skin does not expand along with the rest of its body. When the skin becomes too tight, the spiderling sheds it and grows a new one.

Newborn spiderlings have no eyes, hair, or markings of any kind.

The first molt takes place while the spiderling is still in the egg sac. Males molt five to six times before they are adults. Females molt up to nine times. Females do not look much different from males until the last few molts.

To molt, a black widow spider hangs from a thread of silk with its legs dangling. As it moves its body up and down gently, the hard shell around the cephalothorax splits and falls to the ground. Then the spider wiggles out of the old skin around its abdomen and legs. Now it must expand its body and flex its legs while a new skin hardens. The whole process takes about 30 minutes. Later, the spider cuts its old skin from its web.

As the black widow matures, its colorings change. After its first molt, it is light yellow or gray with an orange abdomen. Its body gradually becomes more brown and then black as it continues to molt. Finally, all that is left of the yellow and orange is a few stripes and dots, plus the hourglass marking on the belly.

CHAPTER FOUR:

While insects eat plants, the black widow survives only on the *prey* it catches in its web. After trapping and killing its prey, the black widow sucks out its juices with its chelicerae. Then the spider releases its prey from the web.

A black widow eats almost anything

Black widows are not picky eaters. They will eat almost anything that becomes snared in their webs. Male black widows do not eat after they become adults. Instead, they leave their webs in search of mates. After mating, they are either eaten by the female or they starve to death.

A female black widow's most common foods are ants and flies. She also eats sowbugs, butterflies, moths, bees, and even her worst enemy, wasps. Animals as large as centipedes, scorpions, and crickets have been known to get caught in the black widow's web. She eats them, too. And she will eat animals with hard shells such as beetles.

A black widow feasts during the summer months when hunting is good. She may even move victims to a spot near her hiding place until she has time to eat them all.

Author Raymond W. Thorp studied adult female black widow spiders in the 1940s. He kept a record of everything they ate during their lifetimes (about one year). According to his book, one ate "240 flies, three grasshoppers, and two garden spiders." Another black widow ate "197 flies, seven sowbugs, and a small centipede." A third one ate "163 flies, two moths, one grasshopper, and one cricket."

But the female black widow can live for long periods of

A black widow expertly traps a ringneck snake in central Florida.

time without eating, too. Thorp kept some for as long as four months without feeding them. The spiders did not die, but their abdomens shrank "like deflated balloons." One time, Thorp lost a jar containing a black widow spider. When he found it nine months later, the spider was still alive. After being given food, she recovered from her fast!

Another researcher, *zoologist* B. J. Kaston, kept young

female black widow spiders without feeding them. The first one died after only 36 days. The hardiest lived over six months.

A web makes a happy hunting ground

Males and young females also hunt using webs. But their abilities cannot equal those of the large and deadly adult female black widow spider.

This expert hunter builds a web carefully, then waits out of sight. Because her eyesight is not good, she cannot see what the web has snared. But she knows when the web has snared something, because she can feel the vibrations with her feet.

When the web has been disturbed, the black widow follows the vibrations in hopes of a good supper. Sometimes she finds only a twig or a leaf. If so, she releases it, mends her net, and hurries out of sight to wait again.

Often a fly or moth is caught in the web. If that happens, the black widow works quickly to make sure it doesn't get away. Using the combs on her hind legs, she quickly throws strands of silk over her victim. This silk is stickier than the silk she uses to build her web. The special combs allow her to do this quickly, even while the silk is still in a liquid state. If the prey gives her any trouble, the black widow can deposit large drops of a gluey material like rubber cement to hold the victim in place.

Sometimes, more than one insect gets caught in the web at the same time. The greedy black widow then works quickly to trap them all. She runs back and forth between victims, tying a leg here and a wing there, until all are trapped in silk and unable to escape.

Often the web and the extra strands of silk are all a black widow needs to trap her prey. She only resorts to a third weapon if the victim is especially large or powerful. In such cases, the black widow nips the victim with her fangs, injecting *venom*. The victim struggles violently for a few seconds. Soon it is paralyzed by the poison and is unable to move.

The black widow keeps a tidy web

Usually the black widow feasts on her prey right away. Afterward, she cuts the threads that hold the victim in place and lets the *carcass* fall to the ground.

If her prey is large enough, the black widow can feast on it for several days. In that case, she usually hoists it up to a spot near her hiding place. This takes the carcass out of the sight of birds or other animals that might steal it. It also leaves the web free so she can catch other prey.

A female black widow watches over her newly created egg sac.

To hoist a victim, the black widow first attaches strong cables of silk to it. Then she pulls on the cables from above with her front feet. She may also push the carcass from underneath with her abdomen to get it moving.

Often the black widow runs up and down her web several times, pushing and pulling a carcass that is much larger than herself. Because the carcass only moves about half an inch at a time, it might take a couple of hours to move it to where she wants it.

The black widow always keeps a tidy web. After she has removed a carcass from her web, she carefully repairs it. Then she waits for her next victim.

CHAPTER FIVE:

The black widow spider has fascinated humans for many years. Many people do not know that black widows are helpful. Because the female's bite is so deadly, however, everyone should know what to do if they or someone else is bitten by a female black widow.

Spidermania

The female black widow has a bad reputation. Because of it, she is a popular character in cartoons, books, and movies.

Perhaps you are familiar with the movie *Black Widow*.

It's about a woman who continually marries and then kills her husbands.

One of the oldest stories about spiders comes from an ancient Greek myth. In it, a highly skilled weaver named Arachne challenges the goddess Athene to a weaving contest. When Arachne loses the contest, she tries to hang herself. But the goddess condemns her to a life of weaving by turning her into a spider.

The Navajo have a much kinder view of spiders. According to their tradition, a mythical figure called the Spider Woman once taught a young girl to weave baskets, water jars, and blankets. The girl then passed on her skills to other Navajo.

People from the Middle Ages believed spiders could cure diseases. Many of them wore live spiders in nutshells or leather pouches around their necks as good luck charms.

A few centuries ago, Italians thought they could cure themselves from the effects of a spider bite by performing a frenzied dance. They called the dance the Tarantella, thinking the bite of a tarantula was responsible for their pain. But the real culprit was probably a member of the widow family.

Early American settlers believed that webs contained hidden messages about the weather and other world events. African-Americans thought the way a spider hung from its web indicated good or back luck, such as the coming of a letter or money, death, or loss of a keepsake.

Black widows can be helpful

Many centuries ago, Native Americans in Utah and California tried to use the black widow's poison against their enemies. They crushed black widow spiders and mixed them along with rattlesnake venom into an animal's liver. Then they smeared the liver on their arrowhead tips.

Primitive people used spiders for fishing bait. They also made fishing nets, bags, and caps out of spider silk.

Spiders are helpful to farmers because they kill insects that damage crops. Many gardeners provide homes for spiders for the same reason.

Many people have tried to harvest the silk of spiders, especially that of black widow spiders. Although their silk is fine, it is strong. Once, 150 yards of silk thread were collected from a single spider in an hour and fifteen minutes. But about 5,000 spiders would be needed to make enough silk for one dress.

Half as many silkworms can make that amount of silk in the same amount of time. Because spider silk is finer than the silk from silkworms, it is more difficult to work with. Also, black widows are harder to keep than silkworms. They cannot be kept together or they will eat each other. So today, silkworms instead of spiders are used in the production of silk.

Many people have tried to harvest the black widow spider's silk, but have found that thousands of spiders are needed to make one silk dress.

The silk from black widow spiders, however, has been successfully used in telescopes, gunsights, and laboratory and surveying equipment. It is fine enough for delicate instruments. Yet it is extremely strong and will last through all kinds of weather. Today, other materials are often used. But some military labs keep black widow spiders on hand for use in repairing older optical equipment.

Preventing black widow bites

The best way to prevent black widow bites is to wear protective clothing when walking in tall grass or other areas where black widows are known to live. Another way is to keep attics and basements clean so black widows have no place to hide.

Many people have been bitten by black widows hiding in shirts, shoes, or stored linens. If you live in an area with lots of spiders, it is a good idea to shake out your clothes before putting them on. Also, shake out sheets and blankets before putting them on the beds.

To avoid black widow bites when camping, always shake out your sleeping bag before crawling into it. Be careful about lying or sitting in a grassy area to rest. And if you remove a jacket or boots while resting, shake them out, too, before putting them back on.

Learn what a black widow's web looks like. That way,

Campers or hikers should learn to recognize the tangled web of a black widow spider.

if you see one, you will know there are black widows in the area. Also, study a picture of an adult female black widow so you remember what she looks like.

What to do if you are bitten

Remember that black widows are afraid of humans. They only bite when they are surprised, or when they are trapped in clothing and pressed against the body.

The bite of a black widow feels like a mild pinprick. Many people do not even notice it. The poison doesn't cause problems at the bite site. Instead, it affects a person's nervous system. As it travels throughout the body, muscles start to cramp. The pain from this cramping may be severe. The poison may also cause a headache, vomiting, or dizziness.

The degree of sickness depends on how much venom the black widow has injected into the body. If a black widow has a full supply of venom and holds on to the skin until she deposits all of it, a person can get very sick and even die. Many times, though, the spider bites but injects very little poison. Then a person's symptoms are not as severe.

If you are bitten by a spider, have someone take you to the nearest hospital. Even if the bite is not serious, you should have a tetanus shot and the bite should be cleaned.

The patient who develops severe symptoms such as stomach or chest pain will probably be given something to relax the muscles. Sometimes symptoms are very severe. A doctor may think the person is having an appendicitis or heart attack. If that happens, be sure to tell the doctor that the person was bitten by a spider.

Few people die from black widow bites today. Children and older people tend to get the worst symptoms. A widow *antivenin* is available, but it also can make a person very sick. It is used only in the worst cases.

The venom from a female black widow is 15 times more potent than the venom from a rattlesnake. Fortunately, the black widow's poison glands are much smaller, so she injects much less poison. Still, many people are surprised that so small a creature can inflict so much pain.

Your chances of dying from a black widow bite are about the same as your chances of being struck by lightning. It probably will not happen. Nevertheless, the black widow is a spider to watch out for.

A female guards three egg sacs. They may contain as many as 750 young.

INDEX/GLOSSARY:

ABDOMEN 6, 9, 13, 15, 23, 24, 27, 29, 31, 36—*The rear part of a spider's body which contains the heart, lungs, and digestive tube.*

ANTIVENIN 43—*A serum that stops the effects of venom poison.*

ARACHNIDA 6—*A class of Arthropods having eight legs and bodies divided into two parts.*

ARTHROPODA 6—*The phylum into which scientists group animals that have segmented bodies and jointed legs.*

BALLOONING 27—*Flying through the air on air currents by means of long strands of silk.*

BRIDGE 18—*The strand of silk that is the main support of a spider's web.*

CARCASS 33, 36—*The dead body of an animal.*

CEPHALOTHORAX 6, 9, 29—*The front (head and chest) of a spider's body, which contains the brain, nervous system, mouth, and sucking stomach.*

CHELICERAE 8, 29—*A spider's special plierlike jaws that include the fangs.*

COMPOUND EYES 9—*The unusual eyes of insects and arthropods, which contain as many as 30,000 six-sided lenses.*

EVOLUTION 6—*A theory that living things gradually developed from earlier life forms.*

FANGS 5, 8, 24, 33—*Two sharp teeth protruding from a spider's chelicerae through which a spider injects its venom.*

FOSSILS 6—*The remains of once-living creatures imbedded in stone.*

GENUS 12—*A group of animals having many similar characteristics, composed of one or more species.*

GRUB 20—*A soft wormlike larva of an insect.*

LATRODECTUS 12—*The scientific name for the widow genus of spiders.*

MOLTING 28, 29—*Shedding an outer layer of skin.*

MUD DAUBER WASP 19, 20—*Any of a variety of wasps that build cells of hard, caked mud for their eggs.*

ORB 17—*Circular; shaped like a sphere or globe.*

PEDIPALPS (PALPS) 8, 23, 24—*The two feelers on either side of a spider's chelicerae.*

PHYLUM 6—*A broad division of the animal kingdom.*

PREY 29, 33—*An animal hunted by other animals for food.*

INDEX/GLOSSARY:

SILK 5, 9, 18, 23, 25, 26, 27, 32, 33, 36, 39, 40—*The fine transparent threads produced by spiders.*

SILK GLANDS 9—*Organs located in a spider's abdomen near the tail, which store liquid silk.*

SPECIES 9, 12, 13, 15—*A group of plants or animals with common features that set it apart from other groups.*

SPERM 8, 23,2 4—*Fluid produced by a male that must combine with a female's eggs to produce young.*

SPIDERLINGS 21, 22, 26, 27, 28, 29—*Newborn spiders.*

SPINNERETS 9, 27—*Tubelike fingers that stick out of a spider's tail through which silk is spun.*

TANGLED WEBS 17—*A web that has a tangled, irregular appearance.*

TARANTULA 10, 37—*A large, hairy spider with a poisonous bite that generally has little effect on warm-blooded animals.*

THERIDIIDAE 11—*The family to which widow spiders belong.*

TORPID 17—*Inactive, numb.*

VENOM 33, 39, 42, 43—*The poison injected by an animal such as a spider.*

VIBRATE 23, 32—*Move rapidly back and forth; quiver.*

WIDOW 5—*A woman whose husband is dead.*

ZOOLOGIST 31—*A person who studies animals.*

13983

595.4
NIE
  Nielsen, Nancy J.
    The black widow
  spider

DATE DUE

OCT 07 1991		SEP 17 1993	
	NOV 05 1991	DEC 1 1996	
		DEC 2 1996	
		MAY 25 1995	
MAR 04 1993			
		SEP 21 1995	
FEB 13 1996			